Jenius
The Amazing Guinea Pig

Jenius
The Amazing Guinea Pig

Dick King-Smith

Illustrated by Brian Floca

Hyperion Books for Children
New York

Printed in the United States of America.

First Edition

1 3 5 7 9 10 8 6 4 2

The artwork is prepared using pen and ink.

This book is set in 17-point ITC Berkeley.

Library of Congress Cataloging-in-Publication Data
King-Smith, Dick.
Jenius: the amazing guinea pig / Dick King-Smith; illustrated by
Brian Floca. — 1st ed.
p.   cm.
Summary: Eight-year-old Judy tries to convince her parents and
classmates that her brilliant guinea pig can do all the tricks she says
it can.
ISBN 0-7868-0243-X (trade)—ISBN 0-7868-1135-8 (pbk.)
[1. Guinea pigs—Fiction. 2. Schools—Fiction.] I. Floca,
Brian, ill. II. Title.
PZ7.K616Je   1996
[Fic]—dc20   95-50633

Contents

Jenius
The Amazing Guinea Pig

/

Chapter 1

"If I were the Queen of England," Judy said, "I wouldn't have corgis."

"What sort of dogs would you have, Judy?" asked her teacher.

The class was talking about pets and which were their favorites.

"I wouldn't have dogs at all."

"What would you keep, then," asked

Judy's teacher, "if you were the Queen of England?"

"Guinea pigs," answered Judy.

Everybody burst out laughing, and Judy turned very red.

"They're my favorite animals," she said defiantly. "If I were the Queen, I'd keep lots of them."

"In hutches, you mean?"

"No. In my palace."

"But Judy," said her teacher, "wouldn't it look rather odd if someone very important came to visit, like, say, the President, and the Queen, I mean *you*, said, 'Please take a seat, Mr. President,' and there was a guinea pig sitting in the armchair?"

"And there'd be messes all over the carpet," someone said.

"And the President would step in them," said someone else.

Everybody giggled.

"My guinea pigs would be housebroken," muttered Judy, close to tears.

"Palace-broken, you mean," said a voice, and now there was so much snickering that the teacher said, "That's enough, children."

She put her hand on Judy's shoulder and said, "It's a nice idea, but even if you were the Queen you wouldn't be able to train a guinea pig like you can train a dog. Only certain animals are intelligent enough to be taught things by humans, and I'm afraid guinea pigs are not among

them. They're sweet little creatures, Judy, but they haven't got a lot of brains."

"You *have* got a lot of brains," said Judy.

As always, she had run to the shed in her backyard the moment she arrived home from school, to see her own two guinea pigs. One was a reddish rough-haired boar called Joe and the other was a smooth-coated white sow named Molly. Judy had gotten them on her sixth birthday, nearly two years ago, and they were very dear to her. Her only regret was that, surprisingly, they had never had babies.

"You *have* got brains," she said. "I'm sure of it. It's just that no one's ever taught you to use them. Now, if I'd had you when you were tiny, I bet I could have taught you lots of things. If only you'd had children of your own. I'd have chosen one of them and kept it and really trained it, from a very early age. I just bet I could have."

As usual, the guinea pigs responded to the sound of her voice by beginning a little conversation of their own. First, Joe made a grumbling kind of chatter (which meant, "Molly, you're as lovely now as the day I first set eyes on you"), and then Molly gave a short, shy squeak (which meant, "Oh, Joe, you say the nicest things !").

Then they both squealed long and loud at Judy. She knew what that noise meant. They were telling her to cut the small talk and dish up the grub.

"Greedy old things," Judy said, and she picked up the white one, Molly.

"Molly!" said Judy. "You look awfully

fat. Whatever's the matter with you?"

Molly didn't reply. Joe grunted in a self-satisfied sort of way.

"I'll have to put you on a diet," said Judy firmly, "starting tomorrow."

But the next morning, when she went to feed the guinea pigs, the white one, she found, looked quite different.

Chapter 2

"Molly!" said Judy. "You look awfully thin. What's the matter with you?"

This time they both answered, Molly with a series of small, happy squeaks, and Joe with a low, proud grumble, as they moved aside to show what had happened. There between them was a single, very large, baby guinea pig, the child of their old age. It was partly white and smooth like its mother and partly red and rough like its father.

To Judy's delight it stumbled forward on feet that seemed three sizes too big, until it bumped the wire of the hutch door with its huge head. Its eyes were very bright and seemed to shine with intelli-

gence. Then it spoke a single word in guinea pig language. Anyone could have told it meant "hello!"

"Oh!" said Judy. "Aren't you beautiful!"

"He gets it from his mother," chattered Joe in the background.

"And aren't you brainy!"

"He takes after his dad," squeaked Molly.

Judy stared into the baby's eyes.

"You," she said, "are going to be the best-trained, most brilliant guinea pig in the whole world. And you're going to start learning right away. Now, then: Sit!"

Of course, when you're only a few hours old, standing can be tiring, but was that the reason why Joe and Molly's son immediately sat down?

● ● ●

That night, before she went to bed, Judy wrote the great news in her diary. She was very faithful about putting something in it every day, even if sometimes it was only a little bit about the weather. But Joe and Molly's baby—that was great news and deserved a lot of space.

Judy's Diary. Privit. June 10th:

Great surprise! Molly had a baby! Found him first thing this morning and I am going to train him. Alreddy he sits when he is told. He is brilliant. He is mostly white like Molly but he has a sort of main like a horse running all down his back and that is redish like Joe. I asked Dad what you call someone who is really briliant and he said, "A jenius. Why?" and I said, "Because that is what I'm going to call my new baby guinea pig" and he laughed but

11

I said, "You just wait. One day the world will know June 10th is the birthday of Jenius."

June 10th was in fact a very good time for Jenius to have been born, because it meant that he was around six weeks old by the time summer vacation began. Now his trainer would be able to concentrate on him without the interruption of school.

During those weeks Jenius had grown amazingly. All baby guinea pigs do, of course, but he had benefited particularly, first from being an only child and so getting all his mother's milk, and second from Judy's spoiling.

Ordinary guinea pigs, for example, might get the occasional piece of stale

bread. Jenius got granola bars.

So that Judy's diary, which had contained daily reports of the progress of the wonder child, read . . .

July 22nd: Beginning of summer vacation. Today I took Jenius away from his parents and put him in the spare hutch. He is reddy to start his training, he is alreddy half as big as Joe, he is alreddy very good at sitting when he is told because that is what I have concentrated on but now I am going to teach him Come and Stay and Down. Joe and Molly don't seem to miss him.

Joe and Molly actually were glad to see him go.

Molly was thankful not to be nagged for the milk she no longer had, and Joe, though at first proud of the obvious cleverness of his son, was growing tired of being patronized.

"Thinks he knows it all," he grumbled to Molly, "with his 'No, Dad, you've got that wrong' or 'No, Dad, you don't understand.' I said to him, 'When you've been around as long as I have, my boy, then

maybe you'll know a thing or two.'"

"So true, dear," murmured Molly. "What did he say then?"

"He said, 'When I've been around as long as you have I'll know hundreds of things.' That little devil!"

"Ah, well," said Molly, sighing. "He's

only young, Joe dear. We're all of us only young once."

"Molly," said Joe, "you're as lovely now as the day I first set eyes on you."

"Oh, Joe," said Molly, "you say the nicest things!"

Chapter 3

"Mom! Mom!" cried Judy, bursting in from the garden with Jenius in her arms.

"Guess what!"

"Not now, Judy," said her mother. "I haven't got time for guessing games this morning with all this washing and the ironing and I've got a lot of cooking to do never mind the housework. Run and play, out of my way, please."

"But Mom, Jenius comes when he's told!"

"Very interesting, dear. Now you go when you're told, there's a girl."

"She just didn't listen to what I was saying," said Judy as she sat on the lawn with Jenius on her lap.

Jenius replied with a small sympathetic whistle, which meant, Judy felt sure, "Grown-ups are hopeless, aren't they? I bet it'll be just the same when you tell your dad."

And it was.

"Comes when you call him, does he?" said her father from behind his evening paper.

"Yes, Dad! Honest! Don't you want to see?"

"Not now, honey, I've had a long day. You go and teach your precious genius something else."

"Like what?"

"Oh, reading, writing, some math. Start with the two-times table—guinea pigs are good at multiplying. Buzz off now, there's a girl."

July 23rd: I think Mom and Dad grew up in Vicktorian days: They think that children should be seen and not herd. I am not going to bother to tell them anything about Jenius any more but only write about him in this dairy so that the world will know how clever he is when I am ~~ded~~ dead and gone.

In the darkness of the backyard shed Jenius squeaked from the spare hutch. "Mom! Dad! Guess what!"

"Not now, dear," said Molly.

"But guess what I learned today!"

"Hundreds of things, I imagine," said Joe sourly.

"No, only one. I learned to come when called."

"Well, now learn to be quiet," said Joe. "It's late."

"Your father's right, dear," said Molly. "Go to sleep now, that's a boy."

Chapter 4

Throughout those fine, sunny summer holidays the flowering of Jenius came into full bloom.

Judy was the ideal trainer, patient and hard-working, and her new pet was the perfect pupil. He enjoyed his lessons, he learned quickly, and what he had learned he rarely forgot. They made a great team.

August 15th: Here is a list of the things I have trained Jenius to do: 1. Come. 2. Sit. 3. Stay. 4. Down. 5. Walk on a leesh. (I do not make him walk to heal because I might step on him so he walks a little bit in front of me.) Before the end of vacation I am going to teach him three speshial tricks: A. Speak, that is, to make a noise when he is told (I suppose I should call this Squeak.) B. Trust, that is, balancing a bit of cookie on his nose. C. Play Dead. He has to lie quiet with his eyes shut pretending to be dead. If I can teach him all these things before the beginning of school I will take him to school and show them all just what a jenius can do.

Every day trainer and trainee worked at their studies. And every night Jenius kept his aged parents awake long after their bedtime, telling them

all the clever things he had learned to
do. He had gotten, it must be said, a
bit of a swelled head.

Molly, who was rather vague by nature,
did not listen very carefully to her son's
boasting, and only yawned and said, "Very
nice, dear" now and then, but Joe became
irritable.

"You must be the most brilliant guinea pig there has ever been," he would say sourly, but this did not improve matters, for Jenius always replied, "I am, Dad, I am," in a voice so smug that it made Joe's teeth chatter with rage.

"That bragging boy," Joe would mutter to Molly. "One of these fine days he's going to be too smart for his own good."

And Joe was right. One of those fine days came quite soon.

Jenius woke early. He looked out of the shed door (which Judy always left open on warm nights) and saw a number of attractive things outside in the garden. There were lettuces and cabbages and the feathery tops of carrots and the shiny dark leaves of beets—all very appealing to a growing guinea pig. Why wait to be fed? he thought. I'll feed myself.

"Mom!" he called. "I'm going for a walk."

Molly came to the front of her hutch and looked across the shed.

"Don't be silly, dear," she said. "You can't."

Joe joined her. "In case you hadn't noticed," he said sarcastically, "there's a door on the front of your hutch."

"Dad," said Jenius in a patient tone of voice, "doors are meant to be opened."

"I know that, boy. By humans. From outside. Not by us from inside. If you can open the door of that hutch from inside, I'll eat my water bottle."

Each hutch had an outward-opening wire door, kept shut by a two-inch turn button, a simple device capable of keeping prisoner every guinea pig that had ever lived. Except Jenius.

Sitting up on his bottom as he had learned, he reached a forepaw through the wire mesh and turned the button vertically. The door swung open, and down he hopped.

He paused at the entrance to the shed.

"Dad," he called, "don't forget to eat your water bottle," and off he trotted.

What happened next was recorded by a short dramatic entry in the diary.

August 26th: Jenius got out and was nearly killed! I am keeping the door of the shed shut in case he escapes again.

Chapter 5

Jenius was sitting happily in the sun-
lit vegetable garden, nibbling a ten-
der young lettuce plant and thinking
what a clever boy he was, when he
heard his name called. He looked up
and saw Judy leaning out of her bed-
room window.

"Whatever are you doing out there?"

she said, and since Jenius made no reply, she issued two commands.

"Sit!" she said, and then, "Stay!"

Jenius obediently sat down, quite content to remain where he was, in easy reach of such nice food.

Judy was just turning away from her window when to her horror she saw the big tabby tomcat from next door drop down from the dividing wall. Slowly, stealthily, he began to stalk the lettuce eater.

Judy thought frantically. If she left Jenius dutifully sitting and staying, he was a goner. If she called "Come!" the cat would surely overtake Jenius before she could get downstairs.

There was only one thing to be done, only one order she could give that might perhaps puzzle the hunter long enough for her to rush to the rescue.

"Jenius!" she yelled in the fiercest, most commanding voice she could manage. "Play dead!"

Jenius, accustomed as he now was to receiving odd orders at odd times, instantly collapsed flat on his side. He stopped chewing his mouthful of lettuce, he closed his eyes, and even the rise and fall of his ribs seemed to have stopped, so lightly did he breathe. He lay, slack and still, looking exactly as he was meant to look. Dead.

"Dead!" said a voice in his ear suddenly.

Jenius's blood ran cold at the sound of this harsh, cruel voice, at the smell of hot, rank breath, at the tickle of long whiskers as something sniffed him all over.

"Pity," said the cat. "Could had some fun if you'd been alive. Ah well, a dead tailless rat is better than no rat at all,"

31

and with that he began to lick at his victim's head.

Try as he would, Jenius could not keep his left eye shut. Under the rasp of the cat's tongue the eyelid was pulled back, and he saw, only inches away, a nightmare face. A merciless face it was, with glowing yellow eyes and a wide mouth filled with sharp white teeth. Despite himself, Jenius gave a little shudder.

"Aha!" hissed the cat. "Not dead after all!" and he opened that wide mouth. But before he could close it again, a clod of earth hit him on the ear and a furious voice yelled, "Scat!" as Judy came galloping to the rescue. She knelt among the lettuce plants beside the motionless figure of Jenius.

"It's all right!" she cried. "He's gone. You can get up now."

As always, she used the system of praise-and-reward by which she had trained him.

"What a good boy!" she said, and from the pocket of her overalls she took one of his favorite cookies and broke off a piece.

Jenius did not move. Now it was Judy's blood that ran cold. Fearfully she lifted the limp body. There was no mark on it, no blood to be seen. Could he have died of shock?

"Jenius!" cried Judy frantically in his ear. "Speak to me. Speak!"

Even though he had fainted with fear at the horror of the experience, the sound of a familiar command was enough to bring him to his senses.

Feebly, through that unchewed mouthful of lettuce, Jenius obediently uttered a single strangled squeak.

It was a much quieter Jenius that Judy replaced in his hutch, and when Molly asked, "Had a nice walk, dear?" he did not answer.

"What's the matter, Son?" said Joe. "Cat got your tongue?"

● ● ●

August 26th: Jenius escaped a horribel death!

Jenius had no intention of escaping again. He had had the fright of his life, and, for a little while, his parents were spared their son's bragging and they could enjoy some early nights.

But before long he forgot, and his natural cockiness returned, particularly when he at last mastered the most difficult trick of the exercises that Judy set him. This was the ending to the trick called Trust.

Not only did he have to balance a piece of cookie on the end of his nose, but then, when Judy said, "Paid for!" he had to toss up the food with a jerk of his head and catch it in his mouth.

Jenius never tired of telling his mother and father how easy this trick was.

"Of course," he said, "I'm the only guinea pig in the world who can do it, I'm sure of that."

"Very nice, dear," said Molly absently.

"Pride," muttered Joe darkly, "comes before a fall."

September 3rd: Jenius has totaly recovered. Tomorrow is the last day of vacashun and I am going to give him a test. I am going to make him do all the things he has been taut and he has got to do them correcktly and I'll give him marks for his performants in each one.

September 4th: Jenius lived up to his name! He performed perfictly and got straight A's and I am going to ask my new teacher if I can

take him to school and show them how brilliant he is and how brilliantly I have trained
him. I'm the only person in the world who
could have done it, I'm sure of that.

Chapter 6

Jenius, it must be said, was not the only one who had gotten something of a swelled head, and by the end of the first day back at school everyone in the class was fed up with hearing how clever both he and Judy were. Before long Judy's teacher too had had enough.

"Judy," she said, "you don't really expect us to believe all this, do you?"

"Yes," said Judy. "It's true."

"Well, I'll tell you what. You bring this amazing animal of yours into school and then you can show us all these tricks that you say he can do."

At once everyone wanted to get in on the act and bring their pets to school.

40

"Oh, can I bring my rabbit?"

". . . my gerbil?"

". . . my hamster?"

". . . my parakeet?"

Until the teacher said, "All right. We'll have a pets' day. You can each bring a pet in to school, provided you bring it in a cage or a box—we don't want anything too big, mind, no Shetland ponies or Great Danes. Who knows, Judy, someone else may have a clever animal, too."

Judy laughed. "Not as clever as Jenius," she said scornfully. "Not possibly. You just wait and see."

Like most people who keep diaries, Judy usually wrote in hers each evening. But as soon as she woke on the morning that had been chosen for Pets' Day, she opened it.

41

September 11th :Today it is Pets' Day
at school! Jenius will tryumph!
* Watch this space! *

At breakfast she could not contain
herself. Till now she had said nothing
to her parents—as she had sworn on
July 23rd—about the progress of
Jenius, but she just knew she would
not be able to resist describing the
success that was to come before
another hour had passed.

"What d'you think is happening
today?" she said.

"You're going to be late for school," said
her mother, "if you don't hurry up. And
clean your shoes before you go. And take
your raincoat—it looks like rain."

"I'm taking Jenius to school," said Judy.

"Very nice, dear," said her mother.

42

"Now, do you want an apple or a banana in your lunch box?"

"Apple," said Judy. "Dad, did you hear what I said?"

"I did," said her father from behind his morning paper. "Will he have to start in the kindergarten or is he clever enough to go straight into your class?"

"Oh, Dad!" cried Judy. "Honestly, I real-

43

ly have trained him." And she rattled off a list of the things that Jenius could do.

"Judy," said her father. "You don't really expect us to believe all this, do you?"

"Yes," said Judy. "It's true."

Her father folded his newspaper.

"Now look here," he said. "Playing pretend games with your precious pet is one thing. But you shouldn't confuse fantasy with truth."

Chapter 7

There was hardly room to move in Judy's classroom that morning.

Everywhere there were hutches and cages and baskets and boxes containing pets. Only Jenius was free, sitting perfectly still in front of Judy.

Judy's teacher saw what seemed to her a rather odd-looking whitish guinea pig, with a crest of reddish hair sticking up along its back, and said, "Is this the genius we've heard such a lot about?"

"Yes," said Judy proudly. "May I show you what he can do?"

"All right," said her teacher. "Put him on that big table in the middle of the room where everyone can see him."

Ranged around the edges of the big table were several pet containers, a couple of hamster cages, a glass jar that held stick insects, and a square basket that had one open side barred with metal rods.

Fate decreed that Judy should put Jenius down very close to this basket and facing it, and though no one else could see what was in it, he could. He looked through the bars and saw a face, a merciless face, with glowing yellow eyes and a wide mouth filled with sharp white teeth.

In fact, the occupant of the basket was only a half-grown kitten, but the sight of it turned Jenius's legs to jelly and scrambled his brains. He was so frightened that he promptly played dead, and there he lay, quite still and barely breathing. He could hear Judy's voice saying "Come!" and then, more loudly, "Jenius! Come!" Then he heard a rising tide of noise, which was

the whole class first snickering, then giggling, and finally laughing their heads off at clever Judy and her clever guinea pig, about which she had boasted so loud and long. But he could not move a muscle.

"The great animal trainer!" someone said, and they laughed even more.

"Perhaps that will teach you a lesson, Judy," said the teacher at last. "He doesn't seem to be quite the genius you told us he was. You shouldn't confuse fantasy with truth."

"How did you do, dear, your first day at school?" said Molly that evening.

"Do you need to ask?" growled Joe. "You were top of the class, weren't you, Son? Got straight A's for everything? Performed perfectly, eh?"

"No," said Jenius in a small, choked voice. "I didn't do anything."

"Well, well, well," said Joe. "The only guinea pig in the world who can do all those tricks and he didn't do anything. I expected you to tell us you did something fantastic . . . hopping like a rabbit, perhaps. Or flying like a bird, I wouldn't be surprised."

Judy came in at that moment with a bunch of dandelions, to hear Joe and Molly making an awful racket. She thought they were yelling for food as usual but actually they were in fits of laughter.

"Flying! Oh, Joe, you are a scream!" squealed Molly, and Joe, snorting with mirth, chuckled, "Pride comes before a crash landing!"

A few minutes later Judy's father, home

from work, put his head in at the door of the shed.

"Well?" he said. "And did our genius perform all his amazing tricks?"

"No," said Judy. "He wouldn't do anything."

"Perhaps that will teach you a lesson, Judy," said her father.

Judy took a deep breath.

"Maybe it has, Dad," she said. "But I wouldn't like you to think I was a liar."

"It's difficult for me not to think that," said her father, "when you tell me such fantastic things. For instance, that your guinea pig can balance something on his nose and then throw it up and catch it. If he can do that, I'll eat my hat, I promise you."

"Watch," said Judy. She took a cookie

out of her pocket and broke a piece off. She opened the door of Jenius's hutch.

"Come!" she said, and he came.

"Sit!" she said, and he sat.

Carefully, she placed the fragment of cookie on top of Jenius's snout.

"Trust!" she said, and he remained sitting bolt upright and stock-still for perhaps ten seconds, till Judy cried, "Paid for!"

Up in the air sailed the cookie and down it came again, straight into the open mouth of Jenius.

"*What* a good boy!" said Judy. "Now you can eat it up."

She turned to her father, who was bending down, hands on knees, watching in open-mouthed amazement, hat in hand. She took it from him.

"And you," she said, "can eat that."

Dick King-Smith has written several terrific books for young people, including *The Swoose*; *The Cuckoo Child*, a 1993 *School Library Journal* Best Book of the Year; and *The School Mouse*, all published by Hyperion Books for Children. His book *Babe: The Gallant Pig* was recently adapted into the blockbuster hit movie *Babe*. Mr. King-Smith was born and raised in Gloucestershire, England, where he still resides.

Brian Floca is a graduate of Brown University and is also the illustrator of *City of Light, City of Dark*, a 1993 *Publishers Weekly* Best Book. His research for this particular project included some close examinations of guinea pigs. Mr. Floca currently lives in Somerville, Massachusetts.